This book belongs to:
_____

Hey diddle diddle diddle

Kate Toms

make
believe
ideas

the cow jumps over the Moon,

when Cat plays his fiddle, Dog sings along to the tune,

Cow's in the bath,

The piggies all prance,

the elephants dance,

the Monkeys start

and, hand in hand, the kangaroos stand,

tapping their toes to the tune!

Hey diddle diddle,

Cat hangs up
his fiddle
and Moon looks down
from on high.

and everyone's waving bye-bye.